THE PRINCESS AND THE FROG

A Magic Kiss

ADVANCE PUBLISHERS

the bayou, magic grows as thick as moss. But it takes a special kind
to see it. I'm old and blind, but I can see things that no one else can
things about the past and the future that no one else knows. I'm a
ecrets—but I'm a storyteller too. My name is Mama Odie, and do I
story to tell you!

One dark and threatening night, there was a disturbance in my bayou. The alligators were going wild—thrashing and snarling and snapping. There was dark magic afoot . . . I could feel it, and all of the bayou animals could feel it too.

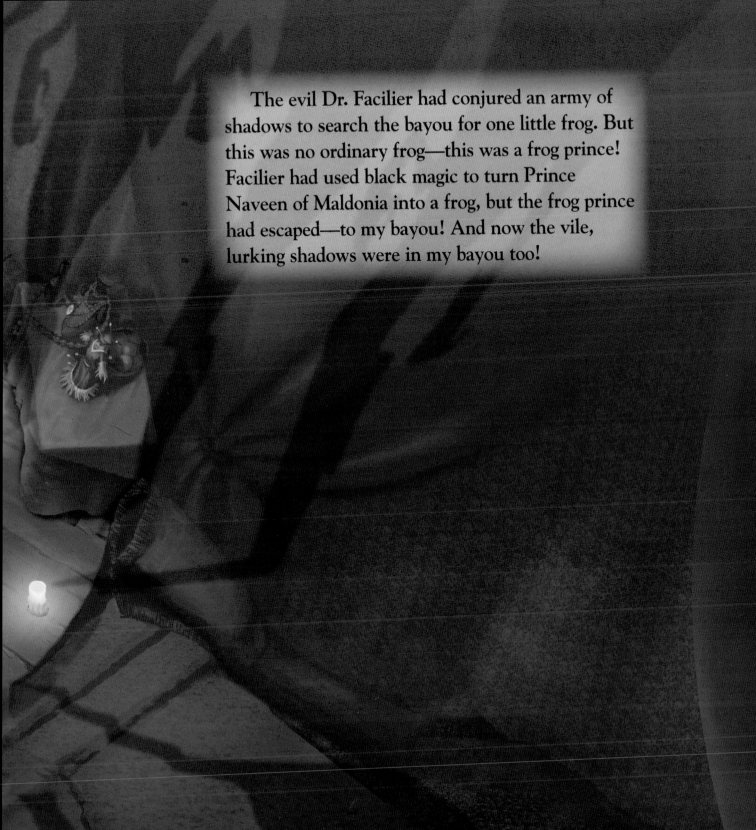

The evil Dr. Facilier had conjured an army of shadows to search the bayou for one little frog. But this was no ordinary frog—this was a frog prince! Facilier had used black magic to turn Prince Naveen of Maldonia into a frog, but the frog prince had escaped—to my bayou! And now the vile, lurking shadows were in my bayou too!

The frog prince and the shadows weren't the only strangers in the bayou that night. Earlier the frog prince had done what frog princes do—he had searched for a princess to kiss him and break the spell.

A handsome Prince!

They were married
And lived happily
ever after.

Unfortunately, Prince Naveen kissed a pretend princess at a costume ball—
(which is not a good way to find a real princess!). Instead of the frog turning
human, the young lady promptly turned into a frog! And now these two inexperi-
enced little frogs were in big trouble in my bayou!

The situation was serious—and I say that as
someone who has seen some serious situations in my
197 years—but I'm sorry to report that Prince Naveen
was not taking things at all seriously. While the shadows
were on their way to the bayou for him, Naveen was
singing and dancing with his new friends!

Tiana, however, was in no mood to dance. Tiana just
wanted to get back to her old life—although I can't say
I'm precisely sure why.

You see, Tiana's life as a human, before the dark magic turned her life upside down, had been all work and no play. Even though she lived in New Orleans, a place where jazz seemed to spill from every doorway and the distant strains of trumpets and fiddles seemed to waft in from the bayou on the warm night air, Tiana never took the time to sing or dance or even listen. She was too busy working.

Prince Naveen, on the other hand, was all play and no work. When he arrived in New Orleans, he didn't need anyone to tell him to stop and enjoy the music. He had gone to New Orleans specifically for the music—the best jazz known to anyone in his right mind.

And now these two completely different personalities—Tiana with her fierce determination and Naveen with his carefree swagger—were together in my bayou. You don't have to be a Mama Odie like me to see that things weren't likely to be . . . well, let's just say that there were sure to be some prickly situations ahead.

Tiana and Naveen were different in many ways, but they did have one thing in common. Neither one of them was very good at being a frog. Trying to catch the same firefly—Thwip! Thwap! Tiana and Naveen wound up completely tongue-tied.

Fortunately, Ray the firefly didn't hold a grudge. In fact, he helped Tiana and Naveen untangle themselves—and then offered to light their way through the bayou. He wanted to take them straight to me for some good magic from Mama Odie.

The bayou was filled with dangers for little frogs.
WHOOSH! Suddenly, three frog hunters caught
Tiana and Naveen in a net!

Once again, Ray the firefly came shining through—he freed Naveen by flying up the hunter's nose! If that's not true friendship, I don't know what is. Then Naveen saw Tiana trapped in a cage, and he leapt into action to save her. Then they worked TOGETHER to get free! Why, those two were starting to become a team!

It was later that the evil shadows sent by Dr. Facilier finally caught up with the frog prince!

Ray tried, but his little light wasn't enough to defeat the shadows. Louis and Tiana fought with all their might, but they were no match for such dark magic either. So I, Mama Odie, decided it was time to step into this particular story. I don't like to toot my own horn (unlike Louis), but FOOM! I zapped those shadows with the biggest flashes of light I could muster. They disappeared pretty quickly.

Fighting off danger together has a way of bringing people…and frogs . . . and friends of all sorts . . . closer together. Suddenly Prince Naveen was sharing in the work, laughing and joking as Tiana taught him to cook. And Tiana was relaxing and enjoying life—even if it was life as a frog.

They were discovering what I, Mama Odie, have always known— that the only thing anyone really needs is the love of family and friends. Everything else—even things we desperately want—like turning from a frog back into a human—comes second.

That night after dinner, Naveen and Tiana danced together for the first time to the lovely strains of Louis's trumpet. I may be old and blind, but I could clearly see that magic was in the air.

And this time it wasn't dark magic—this time it was the sweet magic of the bayou—the magic of friendship and music and love.

Naveen and Tiana were married deep in the bayou. And when the frog prince kissed his princess wife, magic shimmered and swirled and swelled—and broke the spell! As I said, a kiss from a princess breaks the spell! Both Tiana and Naveen were human again!

I've witnessed plenty of powerful magic in my long life—and I expect to witness plenty more over the next 197 years. But this single kiss will surely be—the most amazing magic I ever see!